The Kitten Next Door

Pet Rescue Adventures:

Max the Missing Puppy
Ginger the Stray Kitten
Buttons the Runaway Puppy
The Frightened Kitten
Jessie the Lonely Puppy
The Kitten Nobody Wanted
Harry the Homeless Puppy
Lost in the Snow
Leo All Alone
The Brave Kitten
The Secret Puppy
Sky the Unwanted Kitten
Misty the Abandoned Kitten
The Scruffy Puppy
The Lost Puppy
The Missing Kitten
The Secret Kitten
The Rescued Puppy
Sammy the Shy Kitten
The Tiniest Puppy
Alone in the Night
Lost in the Storm
Teddy in Trouble
A Home for Sandy
The Curious Kitten

The Abandoned Puppy
The Sad Puppy
The Homeless Kitten
The Stolen Kitten
The Forgotten Puppy
The Homesick Puppy
A Kitten Named Tiger
The Puppy Who Was Left Behind
The Kidnapped Kitten
The Seaside Puppy
The Rescued Kitten
Oscar's Lonely Christmas
The Unwanted Puppy
The Perfect Kitten
The Puppy Who Couldn't Sleep
The Loneliest Kitten
Sam the Stolen Puppy
The Mystery Kitten
The Story Puppy
The Saddest Kitten
Nadia and the Forever Kitten
The Shelter Puppy
The Homesick Kitten
The Puppy Who Ran Away
A Puppy's First Christmas

The Kitten Next Door

by Holly Webb

Illustrated by Sophy Williams

tiger tales

For Amelia

tiger tales

5 River Road, Suite 128, Wilton, CT 06897
Published in the United States 2024
Originally published in Great Britain 2021
by Little Tiger Press Limited
Text copyright © 2021 Holly Webb
Illustrations copyright © 2021 Sophy Williams
ISBN-13: 978-1-6643-4060-2
ISBN-10: 1-6643-4060-2
Printed in China
STP/3800/0532/1223
All rights reserved
10 9 8 7 6 5 4 3 2 1

www.tigertalesbooks.com

Contents

Chapter One
The Kitten

"Did you get Christmas presents for Oliver and Tiggy?" Sophia asked, tickling Oliver under his chin. It was the black cat's favorite place for scratches, and he was sitting on the couch with his nose pointed at the ceiling, purring happily.

Zara giggled. "Look—Tiggy's jealous. She wants you to fuss over her, too."

Tiggy had been sitting on Zara's lap, but now she'd noticed how much attention Oliver was getting from Sophia. She got up and marched across the couch to headbutt Sophia's arm and demand her own chin scratches.

"Awww. It's okay, Tiggy, look—you can have right-handed scratches." Sophia petted and tickled both beautiful black cats, laughing at how jealous they were of each other.

"Sometimes I think they love you more than they love me." Zara rolled her eyes. "And yes, we did get them Christmas presents. Mom found these amazing catnip fish toys online—they look just like real fish. Tiggy got a sardine, and Oliver got a trout. Then Tiggy left hers in the middle of the hall floor and my grandma thought it was an actual dead fish. She was worried the cats had stolen someone's lunch. Which isn't that silly because Oliver did once come through the cat flap with a cooked sausage in his mouth that he'd stolen from somewhere."

"You're so naughty!" Sophia told Oliver, but he only closed his eyes and purred louder.

Sophia smiled down at her lap full

of cats and tried not to sigh. Zara was so lucky to have two cats, especially when they were both so friendly and sweet. Sophia would give anything to have just one cat of her own. Her mom and dad liked animals, but Mom said they were too busy taking care of Sophia and her little sister Leah to have pets, too.

"We'll think about it when Leah's bigger, maybe four or five," she'd promised Sophia, but Leah was only two, and it seemed an awfully long time to wait. Until then, Sophia had to make do with loving Oliver and Tiggy—Zara was very kind about sharing them—and stopping to fuss over every cat and kitten she met in the street. She knew the names of all the cats on her walk to school.

"Oh, I can see your mom and Leah coming up the road," Zara said as she peered out of the window. "I thought you were going to stay longer."

"Me, too." Sophia sighed. "I love the beginning of the Christmas vacation, but the part after Christmas really drags, especially when it won't stop raining. There's nothing to do at home!" She rubbed her cheek on the top of Oliver's soft head. "I'd better go and get my coat on."

The doorbell rang, and Oliver and Tiggy leaped off Sophia's lap to see who it was—they were very nosy cats. The girls followed them more reluctantly. Sophia put on her shoes while her mom and Zara's mom

chatted about Christmas, and Leah
tried to reach out of her stroller and
pet Oliver and Tiggy.

"Your little sister likes
cats just as much as
you do!" Zara
said, laughing
as Tiggy put
her front paws
up on the seat
of the stroller
and let Leah
pull her ears.

"Oh, Leah, be gentle!"
Sophia's mom said anxiously.

"Don't worry. Tiggy won't bite,"
Zara's mom promised. "She's very
friendly. And if she minded Leah,
she'd soon disappear. I'm surprised she

hasn't tried to climb in the stroller with her, actually."

"I'm ready, Mom," Sophia said, leaning down to pet the two cats and say good-bye. "Thank you for having me," she remembered to say to Zara's mom. "See you, Zara. Can Zara come over to our house soon, Mom?"

"Definitely. But come now, Soph, I want to get home—it's starting to rain *again*. I think it's going to pour."

Sophia and Mom dashed down the road. They lived on the same street as Zara but at the opposite end, just far enough away to get soaked as they hurried home.

"Oh, come on, come on, where is it?" Mom muttered as she searched in her bag for the front door key while

Sophia bounced up and down to keep warm and jiggled Leah's stroller. Leah was chilly and had started to whine so Sophia turned the stroller around and tried to cheer her up.

"Look at those big puddles! Ooooh, Leah, look—that car's going to make a wave as it goes through. Did you see it splash?"

Sophia turned her head to see if the car went through any more puddles, and caught a glimpse of something pale in the yard next door. At first she thought it was a plastic bag caught in the hedge, but then the pale shape lifted up its paws and shivered.

"Oh, Mom, look! A cat! There's a cat in the yard next door! Actually, I think it's a kitten!"

The kitten obviously heard Sophia call out. Its ears flattened, and it looked around frantically.  Then, unnoticed, it darted from the hedge it had been sheltering under and shot down the side path that led to the backyard.

Mom had finally found the door key in her coat pocket and was trying to get the stroller inside. "Can you help me lift it over the step, Sophia?"

"Did you see the kitten?" Sophia asked, bumping the stroller up while craning her neck around to see if it had come out from the hedge. "It was really tiny, Mom, and so sweet. It was all the colors! Orange and black and white in patches."

"Oh! No, I didn't. That's a calico I think," Mom said. "Come in out of the rain, Soph. If it's got any sense, the kitten will have gone home now."

But the kitten hadn't gone home. She didn't have a home to go to.

Instead, she was huddled underneath a bush in the backyard next door, trying to stay out of the rain. It wasn't working very well. She was thin even when she was dry, and now she was so wet that all her bones were showing through her slicked-down fur.

The kitten peered miserably at
the heavy drops, shivering as more
rain dribbled down the branches and
soaked into her fur. Another huge
drop splashed onto her back, and she
meowed faintly.

Maybe she should go back to that
big old shed.... At least there she had
been mostly dry. But what if people
were in it again, with the boxes and the
noise? She had hidden herself behind
a stack of paving slabs, but when she'd
finally been brave enough to peek out
again, everyone was gone.

Her mother, the other kittens,
everyone.

The kitten had stumbled around the
shed and the abandoned builder's yard

for hours, searching anxiously for her family. They had to be coming back.

When it got dark, she had returned to their nest—a pile of ragged dust sheets in the corner of the shed—but it had been so hard to sleep without her brothers and sisters and her mother to snuggle up with. The shed seemed to be full of noises that she'd never noticed before—the rain drummed heavily on the roof, and the wind shrieked through the cracks in the walls. The dust sheets were chilly and damp now that she was on her own.

In the end, hunger had driven her out the next day. She'd crept under the battered steel gates and padded along the road, foraging for something, anything, to eat. She'd managed to find a paper bag with the end of a sausage roll, but that was all. She was starving. At least the rain meant she could drink out of puddles, but the kitten was starting to think her fur had been wet and cold forever.

She had darted into the yard to avoid a passing car speeding by and sending up a huge, splashing wave of dirty water. She had escaped most of it, but her tail and back legs were soaked.

What was she going to do?

Chapter Two
Meeting the Neighbor

The kitten lurked under the dripping
leaves for the rest of the afternoon
as the rain gradually tailed off into a
damp, gray drizzle. There were noises
coming from inside the house—a
banging of doors and voices—and she
watched nervously as figures passed
the kitchen windows.

Then, after a while, one of the

windows was pushed open a crack, and the most delicious smells began to float over on the misty air. The kitten edged out from under the bush, little by little, sniffing hopefully. She was empty and cold with hunger, and that smell was so good it seemed to be pulling her toward the house.

She padded shivering through the wet grass to the patio. Then she stood at the very edge of the pavement and shook herself briskly so her fur stood out in a hundred little wet spikes. She stared up at the window and measured the distance in her head— the flowerpot to the bench, the seat of the bench to the arm, the arm to the back, and then onto the windowsill. She could do that.

She started to creep across the patio,
but then flinched in fright as a loud
voice spoke near the window and
someone laughed. The kitten froze for
a moment and then whisked around
and dashed along the patio to the
shady path down the side of the house.
She was hungry, but for the moment,
her fear of people was greater.

There were food smells here, too,
which she hadn't noticed when she'd

scurried down the path earlier. Not good smells, like the ones coming from the house, but she found a few food scraps dropped around the garbage can. A grubby, stale pizza crust filled her belly a little, then she curled up to sleep between two of the garbage cans, out of the drizzly rain.

It was a long night out in the cold. The kitten huddled in her miserable shelter, twitching awake every so often as a car sped by or she heard some other creature pattering past.

It was another delicious smell that woke her the next morning—the smell of breakfast cooking. The scent was wafting out from the house as far as her little hideaway, and it was so good that she overcame her fear. The kitten trotted down the path and back onto the patio, and this time she scratched and clambered and clawed her way up the bench until she was perched on the windowsill.

She peered nervously into the kitchen. There was a woman inside frying a pan of bacon—so that was the delicious smell. She was humming quietly to herself, and with the bacon smell tempting her, the kitten decided that maybe this person wasn't very frightening after all.

Then the woman turned around and squeaked in surprise—the kitten squeaked, too, backing along the windowsill in sudden panic.

"Oh, no, don't go, shh, shh," the woman called gently. "Hey...." She

turned off the heat under the pan and
tiptoed to the window. "Hello, little
one. Aren't you sweet? Where did
you come from?" Then she laughed.
"Are you after bacon for breakfast?
You look as though you need it." She
backed slowly toward the stove and
picked up a little strip of bacon from
the pan, blowing on her fingers.
Then she waved it at the kitten,
who was still
watching her
through
the
window,
her ears
flattened
with
worry.

Should she run? The woman was coming closer ... but ... but ... *food*! The kitten couldn't help herself. Before she knew it, she was padding slowly back along the windowsill, peeking around the side of the open window. As the woman held out the scrap of bacon, the kitten leaned in and picked it delicately out of her fingers.

"Want some more?" the woman asked, laughing, and the kitten stared at her hopefully. It was so good. And there was a whole panful, she could see it, just over there.

This time the woman gave her a bigger piece and then a scrap of bread dipped in the fat, and the kitten wolfed it all down.

She was on the inside windowsill

now, perched above the sink. By the time the woman had poured her a bowl of milk, the kitten was crouched on the draining board, eagerly lapping, all her fear forgotten.

Just as the kitten had finished the milk, a man walked into the kitchen, and the door banged loudly. She darted back to the window in panic, and the two of them stared at each other. The man didn't look quite as friendly as the woman who'd fed her, the kitten thought.

"Where did that cat come from?" he demanded.

"She just popped her nose around the window while I was making bacon, lettuce, and tomato sandwiches. She's a sweetie."

The kitten looked on anxiously as the

man took some bacon out of the pan, put it between two slices of bread with lettuce and tomato, and started to eat his sandwich. She was full, but she still couldn't stop watching each mouthful.

"You didn't feed her, did you? Now we'll never get rid of her."

"She's starving, Mark. I gave her a piece of bacon—what's the harm in that? Anyway, you know I'd love to have a cat."

"You're much too soft-hearted," the man sighed, but then he settled down to eating and reading a newspaper, and the kitten went to sit on the outside windowsill again. She wanted to wash the bacon off her whiskers and fluff up her fur now that the rain had stopped, but she did keep peering back through the window. She had never been in a house before, and it was all very new and interesting, but she wasn't sure about the people.

For the rest of the day, the kitten sat on the bench in the wintry sun and went exploring through the grass. Every so often the woman would come out of the back door and pet her. She brought treats, too—a little cube of cheese, a tiny piece of chicken.

The window was closed now but later in the afternoon, when it started to get dark and cold, the woman opened the door again and made coaxing noises to the kitten.

"Louise, are you fussing over that stray again?" Mark said crossly.

"Uh-huh. It's much too cold for her to be outside. Stop being such a grump," Louise called back. "Kitty, kitty.... Come on.... Mark's making spaghetti and meatballs. You'd like a nice bit of meat, wouldn't you?"

The kitten would. She did. And after she'd eaten it from a cereal bowl on the kitchen floor, she followed Mark and Louise into the living room and sat down next to Louise on the couch. She let Louise pet her, over and over, and she purred.

"Mom!" Sophia dashed into the kitchen. "Mom, guess what I just saw!"

"Shh, quietly...." Mom put a finger to her lips. "I just got Leah to go down for her nap."

"I'm sorry, but Mom, I saw that kitten again! The pretty orange and black and white one! And guess what? It's in the backyard next door now! I think it must belong to them—I saw Louise go out and pet it. I was looking out of my bedroom window to see if it was still raining."

"Oh, good, I'm glad it's not a stray," Mom said. "Actually, I think I remember reading something about calico cats—they're almost always girls.

It has something to do with genes."

"So the kitten is a girl? Can I go out into the yard and see her?"

Mom made a face. "It's a little cold, but I suppose if you're quick. Don't annoy Louise though, Sophia. You know the neighbors get grumpy if we disturb them. The other day Mark complained that Leah's crying woke them up in the middle of the night, and I had to apologize. I explained that we deliberately put Leah's room on the side of the house that doesn't join to theirs, but he said they could still hear her."

"They don't like anything," Sophia muttered. "I don't like *them*!"

Mom laughed. "I can understand how they might get fed up with your

recorder practice, though. You did play
'Happy Birthday' over and over last
week. But banging on the wall *was* a
bit mean. So all the more reason not
to mess with their cat, even if she is
cute!"

"Okay.... I'll just look through the
hole in the fence. Louise has gone
back inside now. And I'll put my coat
on, don't worry!" Sophia ran to grab
her coat and her rain boots, then she
hurried eagerly out into the yard.

There was a piece of fence missing
at the far end, where the bottom half
of one of the boards had crumbled
away, and Sophia crouched down next
to it and peered through. It was a little
splintery so she had to be careful, but
she was desperate to get a good look at

the beautiful kitten. There'd never been a cat living at either of the neighbors' houses before! A cat next door wasn't as good as her own cat, of course, but it was so, so much better than no cat at all.

At first, all Sophia could see was straggly grass, but then she caught her breath. Stalking down the middle of the lawn was a tiny cat. She was mostly white underneath but her back was mottled with orange and black patches. She had a white face with a striped orange splash above her eyes and black-and-orange patched ears. She looked a bit like the patchwork quilt that Sophia's nana had been sewing for years—all different colors mixed together to make something beautiful.

"You're a patchwork kitten!" Sophia said delightedly, and the kitten stopped in the middle of the lawn and  turned to stare. Sophia bit her lip— she hadn't meant to speak out loud, and she was worried that she might frighten the kitten away. She looked so little and thin, and very nervous.

But the kitten gazed back at Sophia and then started to march through the grass toward her. Sophia held her breath in excitement.

The kitten was only about three feet away from the fence—and Sophia—when her ears pricked up and she looked back toward the house.

"Kitty! Willow!"

The kitten turned and sped back up the yard, but Sophia was smiling to herself on the other side of the fence. She hadn't managed to pet the kitten this time, but she was friendly, Sophia was sure of it. If only she'd had a little longer.... Still, at least now she knew the kitten's name.

"Bye, Willow!" she whispered through the fence. "See you again!"

Chapter Three
Meeting Willow

The kitten meowed at the back door,
and Louise leaned down to tickle
her ears and then let her out into the
yard. It was still cold, but Willow
didn't mind so much now. Not when
she'd had plenty to eat and she knew
there was a cozy house to go back to
with lots of warm corners to sleep
the night away.

When Louise was home, she was very good about letting Willow in and out, but the kitten had learned to stay out of Mark's way. He never opened doors for her or put down any food or water, and he'd pushed Willow off the couch a couple of times. He hadn't hurt her, just nudged her away. It was easy to tell that he didn't like her very much.

Willow padded through the grass, sniffing the chilly air. There was a bird hopping around on the fence at the end of the yard, and she crouched down to watch it, her tail twitching in excitement. Then a noise from the other side of the fence distracted her, and she noticed the missing board again.

It left an interesting hole, just kitten-sized. Someone had been looking at her through it the day before. Maybe the same someone who was rustling around now. Willow crept toward the fence and peered through the hole. Her ears were flattened sideways, and her tail was just a little bit fluffed  up—she didn't quite know what was going to be on the other side.

"Oh!"

Someone squeaked, and Willow darted back.

"Oh, don't go, please! Kitten....
Willow, hi...."

Footsteps came closer, and Willow
saw the light change on the other
side as someone crouched down by
the missing board. Willow backed
away a little but didn't run to the
house. Whoever it was on the other
side of the fence was making gentle
chirruping noises, and she was
curious.

A face appeared at the opening,
tipped sideways as its owner tried to
look through.

"Hello!" the girl whispered. "Hello,
patchwork kitten. Oh, you're so pretty,
aren't you? I've never seen a cat like
you before."

Willow eyed her thoughtfully and

then stepped slowly forward. The
girl's voice was soft and coaxing, and
she liked it. She rubbed her chin
against the fence and looked at the
girl. Then she padded cautiously
through the gap and nudged against
her knee.

"Oh...," the girl breathed
delightedly. "Oh, aren't you sweet."
Slowly, gently she reached out a hand
toward Willow.

Willow tensed for a moment, but
she allowed the girl to rub the top of
her head and then under her chin. She
closed her eyes, enjoying the attention
and the warmth of the girl's hands.
Very, very quietly, she began to purr.

Every day for the rest of the vacation, Sophia tried to spend some time with the little patchwork cat. She was a bit worried about the neighbors seeing her—Mom had said Louise worked from home most of the time. Sophia didn't want to get into trouble, but she'd never had a chance to make friends with such a small kitten before. And Willow seemed to love the attention, too.

The last day of the vacation, Zara came over. Sophia had spent so long admiring Oliver and Tiggy and wishing she had her own cat—now she could show Willow off to Zara. She kept checking out of her bedroom window, and as soon as she spotted Willow in the yard next door, she dragged her friend downstairs.

"Is she very little?" Zara asked hopefully as Sophia led her down the yard.

"Tiny and beautiful," Sophia told her, crouching by the gap in the fence. "Oh, yes, look—she's still there on the patio." She wriggled back a bit to let Zara look through and called softly, "Willow! Willow!"

"Wow, she really is tiny," Zara said,

watching as the kitten hopped down into the grass—it was almost up to her tummy. "Do your neighbors have her mom as a pet, too?"

Sophia shook her head. "I don't think so."

"She looks too small to have left her mom, that's all," Zara said. "When we got Oliver and Tiggy from the rescue, we had to wait until they were big enough before we could take them home."

"Oh." Sophia frowned but then smiled again as Willow came nosing up to the gap in the fence. "I don't know where the people next door got Willow from."

"We had to keep Oliver and Tiggy indoors until they'd been vaccinated, too," Zara said, letting Willow sniff her fingers and nudge at her knees. "You're so cute!" she told the kitten.

"Maybe they aren't very good cat owners," Sophia said worriedly. "But I can't see me telling them that. They've already complained to Mom because Leah cries too much and they don't like me playing the recorder."

Zara giggled, and Sophia pretended to glare at her. "I'm not that bad!"

"Maybe your mom could mention it," Zara suggested, and then she rubbed her hands together. "Ooooh, it's cold."

"Do you want to come into the back porch?" Sophia suggested. "There's comfy chairs in there, and I brought a ton of blankets out, too. I told Mom we were winter camping, and she said we could

45

have our lunch out there." She smiled down at the kitten. "Willow likes it— she spent a long time sleeping on my knee in there yesterday."

"It's like a fort!" Zara said excitedly as Sophia opened the wooden door and showed her the box of books she'd brought out that morning and the package of cookies Mom had given them to share for a treat.

The back porch was still a little chilly, especially since one of the small panes of glass halfway up the door was broken—Sophia had accidentally thrown a Frisbee into it over summer vacation. Even so, it was a lot warmer than outside, and at least they were out of the cold wind.

They pushed the two chairs closer

together and then wrapped themselves up in a cocoon of blankets. The kitten watched curiously and then stood up on her hind paws, sniffing at Sophia's blanket.

"Come on," Sophia coaxed. She was about to reach down and scoop Willow up when the kitten launched herself at the trailing end of the blanket and clung on with all her legs sticking out sideways.

Zara put her hand over her mouth to stop herself from laughing. "She looks like she has Velcro paws!"

Sophia giggled, and they watched as the tiny kitten mountaineered grimly up the blanket—but Sophia did pull her up the last little bit since she looked so tired.

Willow opened one eye and then yawned enormously. The two girls had shared their food with her—delicious pieces of sausage. She still felt full and it was making her sleepy.

"We have to say good-bye, Willow. My mom's calling us. Zara has to go home." Sophia lifted her down, steadying the kitten gently as she staggered onto the grass. "You should go back to your house, too—it's starting to get dark."

Willow watched as the two girls dashed up the yard, and then she padded through the hole in the fence to scratch at the back door. She hoped Louise wouldn't take too long to come and let her in—it had been chilly earlier on, and now that the sun was going down, she was really cold. She scratched at the back door again and meowed loudly. At last it opened and Willow darted inside, glad for the warmth. She meant to head across the kitchen to her water bowl but then stopped just inside the door, staring around.

What was happening? Everything looked different. The kitchen was full

of big cardboard
boxes, standing
with their flaps
open. There were
piles of stuff all
over the floor and
the table.

Willow backed
toward the door again,
not sure what was going
on. Louise had opened the door, but she
hadn't stopped to make a fuss of Willow
like she usually did. She seemed to be
busy with one of those boxes instead.

Willow watched uncertainly for a
moment, then she began to pick her
way slowly across the kitchen. She
stopped every so often to examine
the piles of plates and sniff at towels

and glasses and pans. It was a huge, fascinating jumble of stuff. Eventually she got to the box that Louise was half inside and decided to see what was so interesting about it. She started to scramble up the side of the cardboard by sticking her claws in, just as she had with the blanket earlier on.

Louise straightened up and grabbed her. "No!" she snapped. "Out of there! I can't be bothered with you now. Sorry, kitten. You'd better go out." She dropped a quick kiss on Willow's head and then opened the back door and dumped her on the patio again.

The door shut before Willow could try to dash back in. She was left sitting alone on the freezing stone pavement with no idea what had just happened.

Chapter Four
The Big Move

"What are Mark and Louise doing?"
Sophia asked the following morning
as she helped Mom lift Leah's stroller
down the front step. There was a big
white van parked outside the house
next door, and she could see their
neighbors and a couple of other people
peering into it. Louise had a big box in
her arms.

"They're moving," Mom explained. "But we can't hang around just watching, Soph. Come on! You don't want to be late for school on the first day back." As soon as they were a little farther away from Mark and Louise and the van she added, "Hopefully the new neighbors won't complain about Leah crying."

"Or my recorder!" Sophia added. Then she stopped in the middle of the pavement, looking horrified. "Oh, no! Mom!"

"What? Did you forget your lunch? What is it?"

"The kitten," Sophia told her tragically. "Their beautiful kitten, Willow. She let me pet her. I play with her in the yard. Sometimes...."

She didn't want to admit to her mom just how much time she'd been spending with Willow. She had a feeling that Mom would say she shouldn't have been tempting the neighbor's cat to come into their yard so much.

"Oh, Sophia...." Mom leaned down to give her a quick one-armed hug. "I know it's sad, but there are other cats on our street. And you get to play with Oliver and Tiggy."

"Yes." Sophia sighed. It wasn't the same. Willow had been so wonderful the day before, snuggling up to her in the blankets. It had almost felt like having a pet of her own. Now she wouldn't even get to say good-bye. Sophia stared miserably at her feet as Mom explained about Mark and Louise's new house. Then she tried to cheer Sophia up by chattering on about how nice it was that they were only back for two days and then it was the weekend, and had Sophia remembered the party they were going to on Saturday? But Sophia wasn't really listening. She mostly just made vague "mmm" noises and thought about how much she was going to miss Willow.

As soon as they got to school,

Sophia dashed onto the playground to find Zara and tell her the awful news. "Mom says that they were renting and they'd been looking for a house closer to work," she explained to her friend. "Dad met Mark last night on his way home. They walked back from the station together, and Mark told him they were moving today. They were packing everything into a van as we walked past on our way to school."

"I'm sorry, Soph." Zara gave her a hug. "You can come and see Tiggy and Oliver anytime, but I know it's not the same as having a kitten next door."

Sophia smiled at her. "Mom said that. Thank you. You know I love them."

"Course you do."

Sophia swallowed the strange hard

lump in her throat. "I just can't believe I won't see Willow again."

When Louise shut the door on her the night before, Willow had been too surprised to know what to do. She stood up and went back to the door, meaning to scratch on it again, but then she remembered the sharpness in Louise's voice. Maybe she didn't want to go back inside, not just yet.

But it was very cold. The wind was slicing through Willow's fur so sharply that it actually hurt. She meowed, wondering if Louise would hear her and let her in. It was only a very small meow, though, since she didn't want to make anyone angry, and it faded away on the wind. There was no answer from inside. No rattling as the door opened, and Louise came to scoop her up and laugh and snuggle and explain it was all a mistake.

Willow peered unhappily into the wind and set off down the yard to the gap in the fence. The wind blew her ears flat, and it seemed almost strong enough to whisk her off her paws. The fence was a welcome shelter, when she finally reached it. There was no Sophia

there to fuss over her, though. The
kitten looked hopefully through the
gap, but the yard on the other side was
completely empty.

She glanced back at the house,
wondering if she should try the door
again, but the cold wind snatched at her
fur, and she shivered. Instead, she crept
into a gap between the garbage can and
the fence and huddled up in a tight ball.

At least she was full. Willow went
to sleep remembering the pieces of
sausage Sophia and Zara had fed her,
the warm blankets she had snuggled
in that afternoon, and the way the two
girls had whispered to her and softly
smoothed her fur.

She was woken the next morning
by clattering and loud voices calling.

She stuck her nose out of her little nest behind the garbage can and shook herself. The cold night had left her stiff and slow, but at least the wind seemed to have dropped. She stumbled clumsily over the grass and up the path that ran down the side of the house, following the noise. She stood cautiously at the end of the path, watching what was going on in the front yard.

Louise and Mark and a couple of other people were coming out of the door with box after box, all those cardboard boxes that had been in the kitchen the night before. Willow flinched as she remembered how Louise had chased her away when she'd tried to look inside one. She didn't want to get into trouble again.

But Louise had let her come in out of the cold and wet only days before. Louise had petted her and fussed over her and whispered to her just as Sophia and Zara had. She'd fed Willow delicious treats. Willow had snuggled next to her on the couch every evening.

Why had everything changed? Willow watched miserably as the boxes were loaded into a big white van and it drove away. Louise and Mark walked back to the house and disappeared inside, and Willow padded farther out into the yard. She stood there, her little patched tail twitching from side to side, wondering what was going to happen. Then the front door banged, and she saw the two of them come out again. Mark strode down the path to the street with his arms full of bags, and Louise locked the door and followed him.

Willow dashed after her. She'd seen Louise and Mark leave the house before a few times, but somehow this felt different. She didn't know where they were going, but she knew she couldn't just let them leave.

Louise froze on the path, staring down at Willow as the kitten wove herself around her legs, purring hopefully. Surely Louise couldn't still be angry with her....

"Lou, come on, we need to get those keys back to the agent!" Mark yelled from the street.

Louise didn't say anything. She looked out toward Mark and the car almost as if she were pretending Willow wasn't there. Then she stumbled on down the path, leaving Willow gazing after her.

They would come back. Willow knew they would. She returned to her little hiding place by the garbage cans and watched. She didn't understand the boxes and the van and Louise's strangeness. She remembered the food and the love and the petting.

She waited all day. But they didn't come back, not that day, nor the next.

Chapter Five
Something Strange

"Hi, Dad! I forgot you were working from home today!" Sophia raced across the playground to give her dad a hug.

"Friday treat," Dad said, grinning at her. "I just stepped out to pick you up."

"Are you taking Zara home, too?" Sophia started to ask, and then she remembered. "Oh ... no—she has soccer."

"Yeah, it's just us. Did you have a good day?" Dad asked as they headed through the school gates.

Sophia nodded. "We've got tons of homework, though, and we've only been back at school two days." She sighed. "Maybe I'll do it tonight and get it over with."

Sophia was telling her dad about how they had to write a diary as if they were a character from *Charlotte's Web*, when they turned the corner onto their street. They could just about see their house from here, since they were on the other side of the road, but it was the house next door that Sophia was staring at. It looked like there was a cat on the front wall. They crossed over, and Sophia started to walk faster and faster. She was almost running by the time she reached their house.

"Slow down, Soph! Where are you going?" Dad asked, stopping at their driveway. "Oh, you found a cat...." He laughed. "That's a cute one. So tiny!"

Sophia was petting Willow, who'd come running along the wall to say hello. "Hey! You're so purry. Oh, yes, you're gorgeous. Who's gorgeous?" She rubbed Willow's ears and then smiled at Dad as the kitten came in close and rubbed the top of her head against Sophia's chin.

"She likes you," Dad said. "Who does she belong to, Soph? Do you know her?" He leaned over and held out his hand for Willow to sniff, but Sophia suddenly straightened up, looking worried.

"I forgot! She shouldn't be here,
Dad! She's next door's cat."

Dad turned around to look at the
house on the other side of theirs.
"What, Mr. Rose? Are you sure?
I thought he had a dog."

"No! Louise and Mark. These
neighbors. This house—the people who
moved yesterday. You must have seen
her before, Dad. Her name is Willow."

Her dad nodded slowly. "Oh, yes,
I remember now. Mom pointed her

out to me. But hang on—"

Sophia stared up at him anxiously. "I know! If they've moved, what's their kitten still doing here? Did they leave her behind? I don't get it—I mean, how could someone forget they had a cat?"

Dad patted her arm comfortingly. "I'm sure they didn't forget her, Soph. But cats are amazingly good at finding their way home. I expect Willow just likes it here, and she doesn't think Louise and Mark's new house is her home yet."

"But how did she get back here on her own?" Sophia said, and then she laughed as Willow tried to climb into her arms. "Oh, Willow! Dad, look— she's letting me hold her!"

"I'd say she's not giving you a choice," Dad said, smiling. "I suppose she must have followed her own scent. I don't know how they do it, to be honest. I remember reading somewhere that cats' noses are almost as good as dogs' noses, though."

"But she's so little." Sophia frowned at the kitten. Willow was snuggling up against her coat now, and Sophia leaned down to brush her cheek over her soft patchwork fur. "She must have had to cross roads by herself. How far is it from Louise and Mark's new house to here?"

"I'm not sure." Dad shook his head. "I don't actually know where they moved to, except that it was closer to Mark's work. I don't have a phone number for them, either."

"We have to tell them to come and get her." Sophia bit her lip. "But how are we going to do that if we don't have their number?"

"You stay here a sec. I'll ask your mom—she might have it." Dad hurried into the house and Sophia leaned against the wall, looking down at the kitten in her arms.

"What are we going to do with you?" she whispered. "How did you get all the

way back here, Willow-kitten? They
should have kept you shut in at the
new house, shouldn't they? I'm so glad
I got to see you and say good-bye,
though. I love it that you just jumped
up for a hug...."

She giggled as Willow started to
scramble farther up her shoulder and
then sniffed curiously at her backpack.
"What can you smell? Does it smell
like school? School lunches and a
stinky PE uniform? Oh! Maybe you
can smell my packed lunch." Very
gently, she unhooked Willow's thin
little claws from the strap of her
backpack and slipped it off. Then she
balanced the bag on the wall and
unzipped the top. Willow stood on her
hind paws and tried to peer inside, too.

"Are you hungry, Willow? I wonder when you set off from your new house. Here you go, look." Sophia opened her lunch box and pulled out the cheese sandwich she hadn't had time to eat. "Do you like cheese? I'm not sure cheese is that good for cats, but I don't have anything else right now. I ate my sausage roll, and you're not going to want a leftover carrot stick, are you?"

She broke off a corner of the sandwich and laughed as Willow lunged at it excitedly. "Okay, okay, it's not going anywhere. Here, look...." She tore up the rest of the sandwich and laid the pieces on the wall next to her backpack and watched as Willow settled down to gobble them up.

"Bad news." Sophia saw Willow's ears swivel as Dad came crunching over the gravel driveway, but she didn't stop wolfing down the pieces of sandwich. "Mom doesn't have their number, either. But she suggested we call the agency that's renting the house."

Dad pointed up at the board, which had appeared in the corner of the yard next door. Sophia hadn't noticed it until now—it said FOR RENT, and there was a phone number underneath.

"The rental agency will be able to get in touch with them and tell them that Willow's shown up here." Then he noticed what Willow was doing and gave Sophia a slightly disapproving look. "We shouldn't be feeding her, Soph...."

"Somebody has to!" Sophia said indignantly. "We don't know how far she had to walk, Dad! Look how hungry she is."

"Mmmm, I suppose so. But she's not our cat. Louise and Mark might not want anybody feeding her."

"They should have taken care of her better then," Sophia muttered under her breath as Dad put the rental agency's number into his phone.

"Oh, hi. Sorry to bother you. I'm from Burnett Street, next door to a house you're renting out? Number thirty-eight. The tenants moved out yesterday, and we've just found their cat. I'm guessing she got out of their new place and came home again. Yes, and she's only a kitten, very small. Could you get in touch with them—let them know she's here? I'm sure they're worried about her.... Yes, thirty-eight Burnett Street. Thanks!" He ended the call and smiled at Sophia. "It's okay, she said she'd call them now."

Sophia nodded and looked down at Willow, who was licking her nose very carefully as though she thought she might have missed some crumbs. Every scrap of sandwich was gone. "What are we going to do until they come and get her?" she asked. "Shall we take her inside?"

"We'd better not, Soph. We don't want her getting confused, and we don't have a litter box or anything like that. Louise and Mark will be coming over for her soon. I'm sure she'll be fine until then."

"We can't just leave her...," Sophia pleaded, but Dad was looking firm. "You've already fed her half your packed lunch, which probably isn't the best thing for a kitten. Come on. Come and get a snack, maybe get started on some of that homework you were complaining about."

Sophia picked up her backpack and followed Dad inside, looking over her shoulder at Willow sitting on the wall. The kitten was washing her paws now and sweeping them over her black and orange ears. She looked very happy with herself, Sophia had to admit. Maybe it was all right to leave her there for a little while....

Sophia kept going upstairs every few minutes to Mom and Dad's room to check on Willow—she could see the wall next door from there. Willow washed herself all over, and then she curled herself up into a little kitten loaf on the wall. Sophia was watching for Louise and Mark's car, too, but she didn't see them drive up to collect their cat.

It was harder to see whether Willow was still there as it got darker—she was just a pale patchy shape on the wall. But Sophia was pretty sure that Louise and Mark hadn't come to get her by the time she went to bed.

Chapter Six
A Celebration

The next morning, Sophia sneaked into her mom and dad's room as soon as she woke up—it was early for a Saturday, but she couldn't go back to sleep. She hadn't heard the neighbors coming to get Willow last night. She'd hoped they might ring the bell and say thank you to Dad. Maybe they had, and she'd been asleep?

Sophia peered very carefully around the curtains. It was only just getting light, and she didn't want to wake up Mom and Dad. But there was certainly no little patchwork kitten on the wall now, and she hadn't been in next door's backyard when Sophia had looked out of her bedroom window. So Louise and Mark must have come to pick her up.... Sophia didn't know whether to be relieved or sorry.

Her hand tightened on the curtain as a flash of color caught her eye. Was that a kitten moving in the shadows under the hedge? Then she jumped and turned as something rustled behind her.

"Soph, what are you doing?" Dad moaned. "It's not even seven o'clock! Even Leah's still asleep...."

Sophia looked at the yard again and sighed. She must have imagined it. There didn't seem to be anything under the hedge now. She dropped the curtains back and came to sit on Dad's side of the bed. "Dad, did you see Louise and Mark last night?" she whispered. "Willow was still sitting on the yard wall when I went to bed, and she's not there now. Did they come and get her?"

Dad sighed and rubbed his hands over his face. "Come on," he whispered back. "Leave Mom to sleep a bit longer. Let's go downstairs."

Down in the kitchen, Sophia stood on a chair to look out of the window over the sink, just in case Willow was in their own backyard. But the yard was gray and empty in the winter morning light.

Dad put the kettle on and yawned. "I didn't see Louise and Mark last night, Soph, but I'm sure they came and got the kitten. Don't worry about her. I expect they'll keep her shut in the new house for a few days, now that they know she might wander."

"I suppose so. I can't see her anywhere," Sophia murmured,

climbing down off the chair. "I'm sorry for waking you up, Dad."

Sophia did all her usual weekend things—watching TV in her pajamas, having croissants for breakfast once everyone else was up at last, reluctantly starting her homework. But she just couldn't stop going to check for a glimpse of a kitten. Wasn't it weird that Louise and Mark hadn't come to say thank you? *She* would have.

She did go out into the yard after breakfast, but no kitten came running to her. Willow must really be gone, like Dad said. She should just get on with her homework and stop worrying.

"Can I wear my purple dress with the sequins to the party?" Sophia asked Mom hopefully when she came downstairs looking for a snack to distract her from her math.

"Won't you be a bit cold?" Mom said, frowning. She was frowning at the recipe for the cake she was trying to make for tonight, though, rather than at Sophia.

Everyone on the street had been invited to a surprise hundredth birthday party for Mrs. Carson, who lived at number thirty. Sophia had been looking forward to it forever— Mrs. Carson was really nice. She loved gardening, even though her daughter had to do most of the work for her now. She was often in the front yard deadheading her flowers when Sophia was on the way home from school, and she always said hello. Mrs. Carson's beautiful orange cat, Timmy, had died the year before, but he had lived to be twenty. She and Sophia liked to talk about all the cats on the street and which were their favorites. Over the last few days, Sophia had been thinking she must tell Mrs. Carson about Willow.

She sighed. "But it's the only sparkly party dress I've got. Can't I just wear a cardigan over it?"

"Okay, I suppose so. Make sure you've got warm tights, too, though— there's going to be fireworks later on, so we'll all be standing outside for a while."

"Fireworks!" Sophia said delightedly. "Oh, wow! I hope no one's told Mrs. Carson anything yet. It's going to be a wonderful surprise."

"She's gone to spend the afternoon with her daughter," Mom said, putting the cake in the oven. "Her family has been planning this for a long time."

Sophia went back upstairs with a banana, thinking about the party and how much fun tonight was going to be. Then she suddenly thought: *fireworks!*

Cats didn't like fireworks. Mrs. Carson had told her they made Timmy wobble like jelly, even though he was such a brave old cat. Zara said that on July 4, she had to plug in a special cat-

calming diffuser for Oliver and Tiggy
because they hated the bangs so much.

It was lucky that Willow had moved,
Sophia thought. She was so little, she
wouldn't know what fireworks were.
She would be terrified.

Sophia nibbled her
banana, thinking.
There had been that
movement under the
hedge.... She could
check outside again
before they went to
the party. Maybe
she'd take a
good look over
next door's
front wall too,
just in case.

Down the passage beside the garbage cans, Willow was still watching the front of the house. She jumped up every time she heard a car go by, but the cars never stopped. When was Louise coming back? Willow had been shut out in the yard a few times while Louise and Mark were working, but never for this long before. It was dark again now, about the time that Mark usually came home from work. The time Louise fed her....

Surely they would be back soon! She was getting so hungry. Willow folded her paws tightly underneath her, remembering the cheese sandwich Sophia had given her the day before.

She hadn't seen Sophia since—maybe she should go into the back yard and look for her through the fence. The girl might have more food. Even if she didn't, Willow wouldn't mind. She wanted company. Someone to pet her and fuss over her. Sophia would let her huddle close and warm up.

Willow hurried down the side path and out onto the lawn, making for the gap in the fence. It was strangely noisy out there in the yard, she thought, her ears twitching in puzzlement. There was a low mutter of voices, the rustling movement of people somewhere close by. She crouched by the hole in the fence and looked through even more cautiously than usual.

"Happy Birthday, Mom!" someone called loudly from a couple of yards over. Then there came a wild and eerie shrieking, like the scream of some enormous animal, followed by a bang so loud it shook the ground under Willow's paws. The air around her seemed to fill with a dreadful flash. What was happening?

She wanted to howl and run and hide, but she couldn't think where to go. Her instinct was to squash herself flat down to the ground in case whatever it was saw her, but the ground was trembling. It wasn't safe. Willow's fur was standing up all over, and she felt her tail swell into a thick brush. She bared her teeth, hissing in terror.

Run? Run! But which way?

She needed somewhere dark and
quiet and safe. Wild with fright, she
darted through the gap in the fence and
raced along the fence line to the end
of Sophia's yard and the back porch. It
had been quiet and calm in there. Her
memories of the back porch were mixed
up with Sophia and Zara feeding her
their lunch and fussing over her. The
back porch meant sleeping wrapped
up in a warm blanket listening to quiet,

murmuring voices. The back porch was safe.

Another huge, thundering firework cracked above Willow's head as she reached the back patio, and the sky lit up with gold and purple sparkles. A few yards away, the crowd gasped and clapped and sighed at how beautiful it was, while the little kitten cringed against the wooden steps.

How was she supposed to get in? She hadn't expected the back porch to be all closed up, just like her own house. She scratched frantically at the door, banging at it with fierce, frightened paws, but it was shut tight. There was nowhere safe to go.

Another shattering bang and then a mass of hissing, fizzing lights. Willow meowed in panic. She half ran, half fell down the little flight of steps that led up to the back porch and crouched in the grass, staring at the door. The firework glow shimmered and flashed in the glass panels—and slowly, slowly, the kitten realized what she was seeing.

One of the glass panes was missing. There was a hole—a hole she could get through!

Willow hurtled up the steps and leaped at the door, scratching wildly, her claws tearing at the wood. She was almost there, heaving herself up toward the hole in the glass, when another mighty bang seemed to turn the whole night white. With a meowing cry, she dove through and crashed to the floor, landing in a crumpled heap.

Chapter Seven
Looking for Willow

"Did you have to put your special diffuser thing on for Oliver and Tiggy?" Sophia asked Zara as they sat in the corner of Mrs. Carson's living room eating birthday cake. It was easily the biggest chocolate cake either of them had ever seen, and it had a hundred candles on it.

"Yes, and we put them in the laundry

room with their favorite bed and extra
blankets to hide under. The laundry
room doesn't have any windows," Zara
explained. "It's much quieter in there.
They'd have been really upset about
those bangs, even though the fireworks
were amazing."

"That's a good idea." Sophia sighed.

"What's wrong?" Zara asked, licking
chocolate frosting off her fork.

"Willow," Sophia said slowly. "I
know Louise and Mark probably came
and got her—they must have, don't you
think? Or I'd have seen her today. But
no one saw them or heard their car. I
can't help worrying that maybe they
didn't come and Willow's still here.
That she was out in their yard with
the fireworks. I went to look for her

just before the party and I didn't see anything, but I keep thinking I might have missed her."

"It is weird that they didn't stop by when they came," Zara agreed. "But maybe it was just too late. They didn't want to disturb your mom and dad."

"I suppose." Sophia tried to smile, but her face wouldn't do it.

"What did the rental agency say?" Zara asked. "Maybe if your dad called them back, they'd know what was going on. It's up to them to make sure everything's okay."

Sophia brightened up. "You're right!" She looked around for her dad and made a face when she saw that he was dancing with Leah in his arms. "I'm not asking him now, though, I don't want anyone knowing he's mine...," she muttered. "And they won't be open anyway. I'll talk to him in the morning."

Everyone got up late the next day— except for Leah, who was super bouncy and still excited about the party. Sophia had to dig her fingernails into the palms of her hands to stop herself from hassling Dad to call the rental agency before he'd had his cup of tea. She just about managed to last until he'd eaten a whole piece of toast.

"What is it?" Dad asked her as he got up to put some more bread in the toaster. "You can hardly keep still, Soph. What's up?"

"I was talking to Zara last night, about the kitten—"

Mom groaned, and Sophia gave her a reproachful look.

"That's not fair! We were only wondering if you could call the real estate agent again. To make sure they got in touch with Louise and Mark."

"Why, have you seen the kitten?" Dad asked, looking puzzled.

"No.... At least, I don't think so....

I saw something moving in the yard yesterday, and I thought maybe it was a bird, but I can't stop worrying. Doesn't it seem weird that Louise and Mark came and got Willow and no one saw anything?" Sophia picked at the piece of toast on her plate. "I mean, maybe the rental agency got really busy and never called them." She looked up at Dad pleadingly. "Couldn't you just check?"

Dad sighed. "I suppose. But it's Sunday, Soph. There might not be anyone in their office." He picked up his phone and scrolled through the recent numbers. "Here we are. Okay. It's ringing."

Sophia nodded eagerly, staring at him. She'd forgotten that it was

Sunday, but maybe someone was there....

"Oh! Hi." Dad waggled his eyebrows encouragingly at Sophia. "I called a couple of days ago about a kitten that had been left behind by one of your tenants.... Oh, you did? We haven't seen anyone come to get her, you see. Oh... Well, that's ... that's a surprise. Okay. Thank you." Dad ended the call, frowning down at his phone.

"What is it? What happened? What's the surprise?" Sophia gasped. "Dad, what did they say?"

"The lady at the rental agency said she did get in touch with Mark...," Dad looked up, still frowning, "and he said Willow wasn't their cat. She was just a stray. Nothing to do with them at all."

"But ... but that's not true!" Sophia sat back in her chair, gazing at him in shock.

Mom put down her mug of tea with a bang. "I was sure she was their cat! Is that really what they said? That she had nothing to do with them?"

"Then that means they didn't come and get her!" Sophia cried. "Willow was outside last night with all those enormous fireworks going off!" She jumped out of her chair and ran

into the hallway to put on her shoes.
"I knew I saw her under the hedge
yesterday. I should have looked harder.
I left her there on her own!"

"Where are you going?" Mom
hurried after her. "Sophia, wait."

"I'm going to check the yard next
door!"

"Okay, well, just wait until I can
come with you. Stay here, Sophia!
I need to get dressed."

Sophia threw her arms around Mom's
waist. "Thank you," she sniffed. "I can't
believe they said Willow was just a
stray. Like it means she doesn't matter.
They fed her, I know they did. She
lived in their house. And then they left
her behind!"

"I know, sweetheart. We'll go and look

for her. Put your coat on and a scarf—it's really cold. The weather forecast was talking about snow." Mom ran up the stairs and Sophia hauled on her coat, then she leaned against the front door, listening to Dad trying to explain what was happening to Leah. Her little sister was starting to cry, too—she could tell that something was wrong.

Mom came down again, and Sophia laughed sniffily at her. "That was quick!"

"Yes, well, I haven't done my hair or anything. Let's go."

"Are we allowed to go in someone else's yard?" Sophia asked, hesitating for a moment at the gate next door.

Mom sighed. "Maybe not officially, but I don't think anyone's going to mind." She pushed open the metal gate, and they walked quietly into the front yard.

"Willow...," Sophia called, crouching down to look under the hedge. She knew it was silly to think that Willow would still be in the same place, but she couldn't help it.

Mom was looking at the path down the side of the house. "I think we can go along here into the backyard. She doesn't seem to be in the front, does she?"

Sophia shook her head and followed Mom down the path. Louise and Mark's backyard looked like theirs, with the same kind of patio and flower beds along each side, but there wasn't much in them. There was no back porch at the end, though. And no kitten came running to say hello.

"Try calling her again," Mom whispered.

"Willow! Willow! Here, kitten...."

Still nothing. They searched under the bushes and behind the garbage cans. Sophia even crouched down to peer through the gap in the fence, but there was no sign of the patchwork kitten.

"She isn't here," she said at last, her voice very small.

"I suppose she might have run off, if she was scared by the fireworks," Mom said thoughtfully.

"Can we go and ask people along the street?" Sophia begged. "Or ... or make posters!"

"That's a good idea. I'll ask on the WhatsApp group for our street if anyone's seen her. Come on, we'll go back inside and you can make a poster on the computer."

"Thanks, Mom." Sophia hugged her tightly. "She has to be here somewhere, she just has to be."

On the back porch, Willow huddled underneath a blanket that the girls had left behind. There had been no more of those terrifying noises, but she still felt jumpy, and she wanted to stay hidden.

She was going to have to move soon, though. She was so hungry. She hadn't eaten in such a long time, and it was making her feel shivery and dazed. She couldn't seem to get warm, and her paw was aching. After she'd dove through the hole in the door the night before, her paw had hurt too much to walk on. She'd dragged herself along the floor and crawled under the blanket, and she'd stayed in the same little heap ever since.

She had to move, the kitten decided, poking her nose out from under the blanket. She felt her fur fluff up at the chill in the air. If she didn't eat something soon, she wasn't sure she would have the energy to move at all. She needed to get back outside and find some food. Maybe she could find Sophia....

Cautiously, she tried to stand up, putting weight on her paw for the first time. It gave way underneath her, and Willow let out a thin wail of pain.

She couldn't even walk. So how was she going to scramble her way back up to the broken pane in the door? How was she going to get out?

Chapter Eight
Safe at Last

Sophia went to bed that night exhausted. She'd gone all along the street so many times, calling for Willow, and they'd put up posters everywhere. She wanted everyone to know that Willow wasn't "just a stray," that she mattered.

She was tired from being so angry, too. There was a seething ball of fury inside her—and she wasn't only angry with Louise and Mark, she was angry with herself, too, for not figuring out what had happened. The fury seemed to have sucked all the energy out of her. She wasn't going to be able to sleep, though—how could she when she was so worried? When Willow was out there somewhere, scared and alone?

Then she woke up shivering and realized she must have fallen asleep eventually—but now she'd kicked half her comforter off. What had woken her? Sophia had a faint memory of hearing crying, but she couldn't hear Leah now.

She'd been dreaming—a strange, horrible dream full of winding roads she had to hurry down because she was looking for something, something that was always just ahead of her, around the next corner. Sophia grabbed her comforter and pulled it up around her shoulders. It was so cold. Mom had said it might snow. Sophia sniffed—if there was snow, poor Willow would be out in it.

She climbed out of bed and stumbled over to the window, wrapped in her comforter like a plump caterpillar. It was so dark out in the yard that she couldn't see whether it was snowing or not, even when she pressed her nose against the icy glass. Sophia shuddered and opened the window. She peered out, feeling the freezing wind strike her nose and the tips of her ears. No snow, not yet. But Willow was still outside, trying to shelter from that biting cold.

Miserably, Sophia shuffled back a little, ready to pull the window closed, when she heard a soft cry—the same sound that had woken her a few minutes earlier. She turned her head, blinking in sleepy surprise. She had thought it was Leah, but there was no sound from her little sister's room now.

The crying was coming from outside.

She stuck her head back out of the window, forgetting about the cold, forgetting about the comforter trailing around her feet. There it was again! A sad, quiet little noise. As if the person making it didn't think that anyone was listening.

Not a cry, Sophia realized. A meow.

"Willow!" she whispered. Willow was somewhere in the yard!

Sophia peered through the darkness, trying to spot a gleam of white fur in the moonlight, but she couldn't see Willow anywhere.

"You're not staying out there," she whispered into the night. "Not when it's about to snow. You're just not."

Sophia dropped the comforter and grabbed her thick fleece top from the chair by her bed. She looked around her room, trying to remember when she'd last seen a flashlight—there was one in the drawer in the kitchen, she thought.

She paused outside Mom and Dad's room for a moment, wondering if she should wake them. Mom had been so upset about Willow. Then again, Sophia wasn't exactly certain where Willow was, and Mom and Dad still got woken up during the night by Leah. Her little sister would crawl into their bed if she wanted company, or Sophia's bed sometimes. Mom and Dad weren't going to be happy about Sophia waking them up, too. And Willow was used to just her. She didn't want to scare the kitten away.

Sophia crept on past and headed down the stairs, her breath catching every time they squeaked. She grabbed her coat and her sneakers and then tiptoed into the kitchen to look for the flashlight. The only light came from the clocks on the microwave and the oven—a faint, eerie, greenish light—but luckily she could feel the heavy flashlight inside the drawer. Then cautiously, quietly, she turned the key in the lock on the back door. It clicked and she froze for a moment, waiting to hear footsteps up above.

Nothing. Sophia eased the door open and looked out into the dark yard. It was so black and silent that she almost turned back, but she clicked on the flashlight instead. She drew in a gasp of breath as it lit up the grass and hurriedly pointed it down at her feet, just in case

Mom or Dad woke up and noticed the glow. Then she stepped out onto the patio, trying not to shiver, and shone the flashlight toward the flower beds.

"Willow!" she called in a low voice.

There was silence for a moment, but Sophia was sure that it was a listening kind of silence. She swallowed hard, trying to tell herself that it was Willow, not something horrible lurking behind Leah's little swing.

Then she heard it again—meowing! It was coming from farther down the yard. Sophia forgot to be scared and half ran across the grass toward the back porch. She shone the flashlight through the glass panes in the door and jumped a little as it reflected back from round green eyes.

"You're there," she whispered.
"I wasn't sure we'd ever find you."
She fumbled at the latch with frozen
fingers and pulled the door open
at last, laughing at the kitten half
wrapped up in a blanket. "How long
have you been in there? Oh, Willow!"

Sophia crouched down and then
caught her breath as Willow hopped
and wobbled toward her. "You're hurt!
Did you have to jump through that

broken pane in the door?" As gently as she could, she lifted Willow, scooping her up in the blanket. "Come on. I don't know how to fix your paw, but at least you can get warm. And there must be something in the fridge you'll like."

Sophia stepped carefully out of the back porch and shivered as the cold air hit her. In the light of her flashlight, she could just see the first snowflakes twirling lazily down and starting to settle on the frozen grass. She walked back up the yard with her arms full of blanket, and she couldn't stop smiling.

Willow watched cautiously from her nest of blanket on the table as Sophia investigated the fridge.

"Tuna! I knew Dad had a tuna sandwich yesterday."

A delicious fishy smell wafted out of the plastic tub, and Willow wriggled herself forward eagerly, almost forgetting not to put any weight on her paw because she was so hungry.

"Oh, I was going to put it on a plate, but that's fine. I suppose there isn't much there anyway."

Willow buried her face in the tub, snatching huge mouthfuls of fish. Now that there was food in front of her, she seemed to realize just how desperately hungry she was. The tuna was gone in seconds, and she licked the delicious juice from around the edges and then from her whiskers.

She looked eagerly
at the little bowl
that Sophia had
put down next to
her, but it was
only water.
She took a
few mouthfuls
anyway and then
gave a delicious shiver. Her paw still
ached, but she felt so much better.

"I think if I give you anything else
you might be sick. And I'm not sure
what else we have that's good for cats.
Maybe...." Sophia ran one finger over
the kitten's head, and Willow heard
her voice shake a little. "Maybe Mom
and Dad can buy some cat food. I don't
know what we're going to do with you,

but even if you have to go to a rescue
center, you'll need some breakfast. I can
run to the store in the morning."

Carefully, she gathered up the blanket
again, and Willow peered curiously
over the top of it as they headed up the
stairs—the food was making her sleepy.

When Sophia huddled the blanket
into a little nest on her bed, Willow
stretched out and then curled back
up into a ball, loving the warmth. She
could feel Sophia snuggling in next to
her and she let out a tiny, exhausted
purr.

"I suppose I should tell Mom and
Dad that I've found you," she heard
Sophia whisper. "But ... I don't want to.
Just for tonight, I'm going to pretend
that you're mine."

A few hours later, Willow woke up as the comforter slid sideways and looked over the edge of her blanket nest. The room was full of pale grayish light, and another face was staring at her from the foot of the bed, a face that seemed to be all wide, round eyes.

"Kitten!" the tiny girl whispered, and Willow flattened her ears anxiously. But the child only whispered again, her voice full of delight, "Night night, kitten...." Then she carefully pulled the corner of the comforter over herself, curled around Willow, and closed her eyes.

Willow watched her for a moment, but she really did seem to be asleep— and so was Sophia. The small one was wonderfully warm, huddled up around her. It was almost like being back in a nest of kittens, now that she had girls on both sides. Willow yawned and wriggled in a little closer.

"Oh, there you are, Leah! Sophia, it's time to get up, love. You need to look out of the window, it snowed last night! And did you even know Leah was in bed with you?"

Sophia pushed herself up on her elbows, blinking and trying to remember. Last night—had last night actually happened? Was it just another dream?

"Look, Mommy!" Leah reached out to grab Mom's hand and then moved a fold of the blanket that was nested at the edge of the bed. "Kitten!"

Not a dream....

Sophia watched Mom's eyes widen in shock. "Sophia! Where did she come from?"

"The back porch." Sophia struggled with a huge yawn. "Ohhh ... sorry. She was trapped in there, Mom. I think she must have climbed inside to get away from the fireworks."

"But ... but when did you find her?" Mom perched on the end of the bed, looking bewildered, while Leah babbled happily about the kitten.

"Last night," Sophia admitted. "I heard meowing, and I thought it had to be her. I did put my coat on," she told her mom, hoping she wouldn't be too upset, but luckily Mom seemed too surprised to be angry. "She was limping—I think she might have hurt her paw."

Sophia tickled Willow under the chin, and the kitten stretched a little and opened her eyes. Then Sophia looked up at Mom. "What are we going to do? Is there a rescue center we can take her to? They'd know how to take care of her paw, wouldn't they?"

"Yes...." Mom said thoughtfully. "Look, we'll talk about it downstairs, Soph. You'd better get your school uniform on. Leah, come on, sweetheart, let's get dressed. Bring Willow with you, Sophia, okay?"

Sophia nodded and then tucked the blanket back around Willow while she found her clothes. The kitten looked so sweet, with just her black and orange ears poking out. "You can take that blanket to the rescue center," she whispered as she pulled on her cardigan. "Then you'll have something to remember us by."

Dad glanced up from the kettle when Sophia walked into the kitchen carrying Willow. He looked upset, but Sophia was almost sure he wasn't really.

"I can't believe you went out in the middle of the night!"

"I'm sorry, Dad...."

"Let me see her.... Mom said her paw's hurt?"

Sophia laid the blanket down on the kitchen table, and they watched as Willow looked curiously around and tried to stand up. Her paw still looked wobbly.

"Hmm. I suppose we'd better call the vet. I wonder what time they open."

Sophia nodded and then swung around to stare at Dad. "The vet? Not ... not the rescue center?"

Mom came into the kitchen, carrying Leah. "I don't think I could send her to a rescue now, Soph," she said, giving her a quick hug while Leah squeaked and waved at the kitten on the table.

"We can't let her be abandoned twice," Dad agreed.

"You mean it?" Sophia felt her voice shake. Willow looked up at her curiously and hopped across the table to nuzzle against her hand. "We really can keep her?"

"You and Leah were curled up around her when I came in this morning." Mom laughed. "She looked so cozy. Like she belonged."

Sophia slipped her fingers around Willow, holding her as if she were made of china, and felt the kitten's sides tremble with purrs.

"Did you hear that, Willow?" she whispered. "You belong to us."